CHILDHOOD FEARS AND ANXIETIES

SEPARATION ANXIETY

CHILDHOOD FEARS AND ANXIETIES

Anxiety and Fear in Daily Life

Catastrophes

Crime and Terrorism

Family Fears

Medical Fears

Nighttime Fears

Phobias

School Fears

Separation Anxiety

Social Fears

Symptoms and Treatments of Anxiety Disorders

CHILDHOOD FEARS AND ANXIETIES

SEPARATION ANXIETY

H.W. POOLE

SERIES CONSULTANT
ANNE S. WALTERS, Ph.D.

Emma Pendleton Bradley Hospital

Warren Alpert Medical School of Brown University

MASON CREST

S

Mason Crest
450 Parkway Drive, Suite D
Broomall, PA 19008
www.masoncrest.com

MTM Publishing, Inc.
435 West 23rd Street, #8C
New York, NY 10011
www.mtmpublishing.com

President: Valerie Tomaselli
Vice President, Book Development: Hilary Poole
Designer: Annemarie Redmond
Copyeditor: Peter Jaskowiak
Editorial Assistant: Leigh Eron

Series ISBN: 978-1-4222-3721-2
Hardback ISBN: 978-1-4222-3730-4
E-Book ISBN: 978-1-4222-8063-8

Library of Congress Cataloging-in-Publication Data
Names: Poole, Hilary W., author.
Title: Separation anxiety / by H.W. Poole; series consultant, Anne S. Walters, Ph.D., Emma Pendleton Bradley Hospital, Alpert Medical School/Brown University.
Description: Broomall, PA: Mason Crest, [2018] | Series: Childhood fears and anxieties | Audience: Age 12+ | Audience: Grade 7 to 8. | Includes index.
Identifiers: LCCN 2017000399 (print) | LCCN 2017005219 (ebook) | ISBN 9781422237304 (hardback: alk. paper) | ISBN 9781422280638 (ebook)
Subjects: LCSH: Separation anxiety in children—Juvenile literature.
Classification: LCC HQ755.85 .P664 2018 (print) | LCC HQ755.85 (ebook) | DDC 155.4—dc23
LC record available at https://lccn.loc.gov/2017000399

Printed and bound in the United States of America.

First printing
9 8 7 6 5 4 3 2 1

TABLE OF CONTENTS

Key Icons to Look for:

Words to Understand: These words with their easy-to-understand definitions will increase the reader's understanding of the text, while building vocabulary skills.

Sidebars: This boxed material within the main text allows readers to build knowledge, gain insights, explore possibilities, and broaden their perspectives by weaving together additional information to provide realistic and holistic perspectives.

Educational Videos: Readers can view videos by scanning our QR codes, which will provide them with additional educational content to supplement the text. Examples include news coverage, moments in history, speeches, iconic sports moments, and much more.

Text-Dependent Questions: These questions send the reader back to the text for more careful attention to the evidence presented there.

Research Projects: Readers are pointed toward areas of further inquiry connected to each chapter. Suggestions are provided for projects that encourage deeper research and analysis.

Series Glossary of Key Terms: This back-of-the-book glossary contains terminology used throughout the series. Words found here increase the reader's ability to read and comprehend higher-level books and articles in this field.

SERIES INTRODUCTION

Who among us does not have memories of an intense childhood fear? Fears and anxieties are a part of *every* childhood. Indeed, these fears are fodder for urban legends and campfire tales alike. And while the details of these legends and tales change over time, they generally have at their base predictable childhood terrors such as darkness, separation from caretakers, or bodily injury.

We know that fear has an evolutionary component. Infants are helpless, and, compared to other mammals, humans have a very long developmental period. Fear ensures that curious children will stay close to caretakers, making them less likely to be exposed to danger. This means that childhood fears are adaptive, making us more likely to survive, and even thrive, as a species.

Unfortunately, there comes a point when fear and anxiety cease to be useful. This is especially problematic today, for there has been a startling increase in anxiety among children and adolescents. In fact, 25 percent of 13- to 18-year-olds now have mild to moderate anxiety, and the *median* age of onset for anxiety disorders is just 11 years old.

Why might this be? Some say that the contemporary United States is a nation preoccupied with risk, and it is certainly possible that our children are absorbing this preoccupation as well. Certainly, our exposure to potential threats has never been greater. We see graphic images via the media and have more immediate news of all forms of disaster. This can lead our children to feel more vulnerable, and it may increase the likelihood that they respond with fear. If children based their fear on the news that they see on Facebook or on TV, they would dramatically overestimate the likelihood of terrible things happening.

As parents or teachers, what do we do about fear? As in other areas of life, we provide our children with guidance and education on a daily basis. We teach them about the signs and feelings of fear. We discuss and normalize typical fear reactions, and support them in tackling difficult situations despite fear. We explain—and demonstrate by example—how to identify "negative thinking traps" and generate positive coping thoughts instead.

But to do so effectively, we might need to challenge some of our own assumptions about fear. Adults often assume that they must protect their children from fear and help them to avoid scary situations, when sometimes the best course is for the child to face the fear and conquer it. This is counterintuitive for many adults: after all, isn't it our job to reassure our children and help them feel better? Yes, of course! Except when it isn't. Sometimes they need us to help them confront their fears and move forward anyway.

That's where these volumes come in. When it comes to fear, balanced information is critical. Learning about fear as it relates to many different areas can help us to help our children remember that although you don't choose whether to be afraid, you do choose how to handle it. These volumes explore the world of childhood fears, seeking to answer important questions: How much is too much? And how can fear be positive, functioning to mobilize us in the face of danger?

Fear gives us the opportunity to step up and respond with courage and resilience. It pushes us to expand our sphere of functioning to areas that might feel unfamiliar or risky. When we are a little nervous or afraid, we tend to prepare a little more, look for more information, ask more questions—and all of this can function to help us expand the boundaries of our lives in a positive direction. So, while fear might *feel* unpleasant, there is no doubt that it can have a positive outcome.

Let's teach our children that.

—Anne Walters, Ph.D.
Chief Psychologist, Emma Pendleton Bradley Hospital
Clinical Associate Professor,
Alpert Medical School of Brown University

WATCH
CAUTION
USE DEF ONLY

CHAPTER ONE

WHAT IS SEPARATION ANXIETY?

Sometimes your parents probably do things that make you unhappy, like take away your phone. Other times they make you do things that don't make you very happy, either, like clean your room. But parents don't do those things because they want you to be unhappy. They do them because they believe that a little bit of unhappiness now is going to make you a better, happier person in the long run. Most parents secretly hate having to punish you or make you do stuff you don't like. But they know that there are some bad parts of life that are also *expected* parts of life.

One expected—and not fun—part of life is occasionally feeling anxious or afraid. Being a bit nervous sometimes is not bad. Much like putting down your phone or cleaning your room, some occasional anxiety may make you a healthier, happier person in the long run.

attachment: the feeling of wanting to be around someone you care about.

inconsolable: so upset that nothing makes you feel better.

intimidating: scary, in the sense of being overwhelmed.

phase: a distinct period with a beginning and an end.

Separation anxiety is the fear of being apart from someone who is important to you. And to a certain extent, it is totally normal. Most little kids go through a **phase** of separation anxiety when their caregivers are not around. However, if separation anxiety continues long after a little kid has turned into a big one, those nervous feelings can become a problem.

IS IT A PHASE?

The classic example of separation anxiety is a one-year-old girl screaming her head off when being dropped off at day care. The weeping makes her mom feel horrible. And yet this form of separation anxiety is actually a good sign! It means that the

Little kids sometimes cry when Mom leaves because they can't understand that she'll be right back.

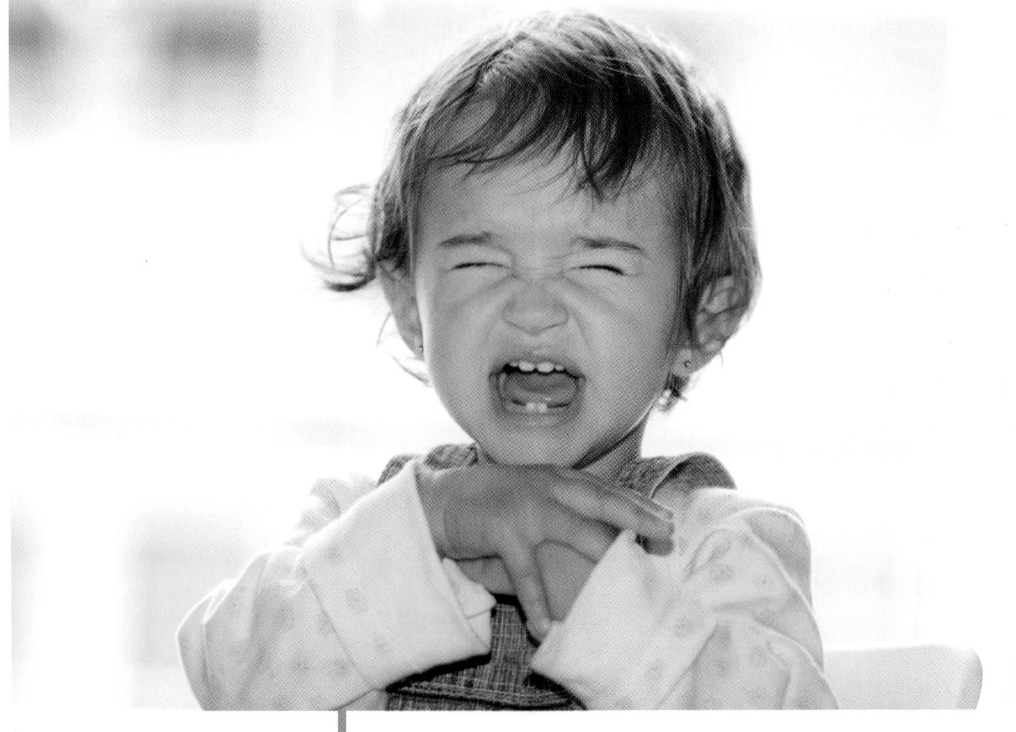

PARENTS AND OTHERS

A key part of separation anxiety is the idea of **attachment**. When two objects are attached to each other, they are physically fastened to one another in some way. When we talk about two people being "attached," we mean it in a more emotional sense. Being attached to someone means you care about that person and you miss that person when he or she is not around.

The phrase *attachment figure* refers to the person someone is attached to. When it comes to little kids, their moms are usually their first attachment figure, with their dads running a close second. Sometimes that's reversed, however, and other times the attachment figure is not a biological parent at all. Not all kids grow up around their biological moms and dads. But that doesn't mean those kids don't have attachment figures who are just as important. Maybe it's an adoptive parent or a foster parent, or maybe it's a grandparent or some other family member. The truth is, an attachment figure doesn't need to be a biological relative. The relationship is what matters.

child is developing normally. She loves her mom and wants to be with her. This is all good stuff, even though it doesn't feel very good when it's happening. As time passes, the little girl will realize that day care doesn't last forever. The little girl stops crying so much because she realizes that Mom always comes back at the end of the day.

All kids are different, and so are their reactions to separation. A lot of it depends on the child's personality. Some kids are only mildly bothered by separation anxiety, and they can be easily cheered up. With just a bit of distraction, these more "mellow" kids quickly get over being upset that Mom left for work.

Kids with more worried personalities might be harder to distract. They feel miserable, even **inconsolable,** for a while. There are babies who panic when Mom simply *leaves the room*, never mind leaves the house! This is tough on the rest of the family. But even these kids usually grow out of their anxiety in time. There are steps families can take to help make the process easier, and later in the book we will talk about what parents and siblings can do to make little ones feel more secure.

The exact timing of separation anxiety can also vary from child to child. It can begin anywhere from about eight months old to about two years old. And it often comes back when school starts, around four or five years old. Going out on your own—even to a friendly place like a nursery school or kindergarten—can be very **intimidating** for little kids. Sometimes separation anxiety is kicked off by a big life change, like starting day care or moving to a new house. But this is a natural part of life, and most of the time, the anxiety goes away on its own. Chances are good that you went through this yourself at some point but barely remember it now. You may not remember it at all!

Here is a video with more information about separation anxiety in teens.

IS IT A PROBLEM?

There are instances where separation anxiety does become a problem. The condition called *separation anxiety disorder* involves fear and anxiety that goes well beyond what is typical for the person's age. People with the disorder feel extreme worry and even panic about being away from their homes or their attachment figures.

Separation anxiety disorder is a problem because it keeps you from fully participating in life.

SYMPTOMS OF SEPARATION ANXIETY

Separation anxiety has a number of symptoms. Here are some of them.

In babies:

- crying
- excessive clinging
- tantrums

In older kids:

- scary thoughts about bad things happening
- refusal to be alone
- refusal to go to school
- difficulty separating from attachment figure
- difficulty sleeping
- nightmares
- stomachaches, headaches, and other physical problems

Anticipating an event that involves separation (such as the first day of school) can make it hard to fall asleep.

To be called a "disorder," the anxiety has to interfere with the daily life of the person. A girl with separation anxiety disorder might refuse to go to school, for example. Or, if she does go, she might find it impossible to concentrate. She keeps worrying about something bad happening—what if her house burns down, or if someone hurts her dad, or if she gets kidnapped on the way home from school . . . and so on. Her anxiety has taken charge of her life.

Separation anxiety disorder can crop up at any age. It's most common among kids under the age of 11, affecting about 5 percent of American kids in that age group. It also tends to happen more to girls than boys. Teens and adults can also develop separation anxiety disorder, but that's less common. Frequently, teens who struggle with anxiety in general will experience separation anxiety, especially when a big transition is coming up, such starting as a new school.

Ask your own attachment figure (could be a parent, relative, or former babysitter) what you were like when you were little. Did you show any separation anxiety? Was it ever a problem? What did your attachment figure do about it? Write a paragraph about what you learned.

TEXT-DEPENDENT QUESTIONS

1. What is attachment?
2. What is the difference between separation anxiety and separation anxiety disorder?
3. Roughly, what percentage of kids have separation anxiety disorder?

CHAPTER TWO

UNDERSTANDING CHILD DEVELOPMENT

Humans are unique animals in a lot of ways. We are the only creatures to have invented skyscrapers and Cheez Whiz, for example. But some aspects of our uniqueness are not quite as obvious.

When most animals are born, they are ready to look after themselves pretty quickly. A foal will try to walk within minutes after birth. Or think about sea turtles, which hatch on beaches and have to make it to the water all by themselves without getting lost or eaten. Even baby primates, like monkeys, are better prepared to take care of themselves than human babies are. In fact, some scientists have estimated that a human baby would need to stay in the womb for almost two years in order to be born as developed as a chimpanzee baby.

WORDS TO UNDERSTAND

cognitive: relating to the brain and thought.

communal: relating to a community.

efficient: relating to the most direct and least wasteful way of doing something.

milestone: an event that marks a stage in development.

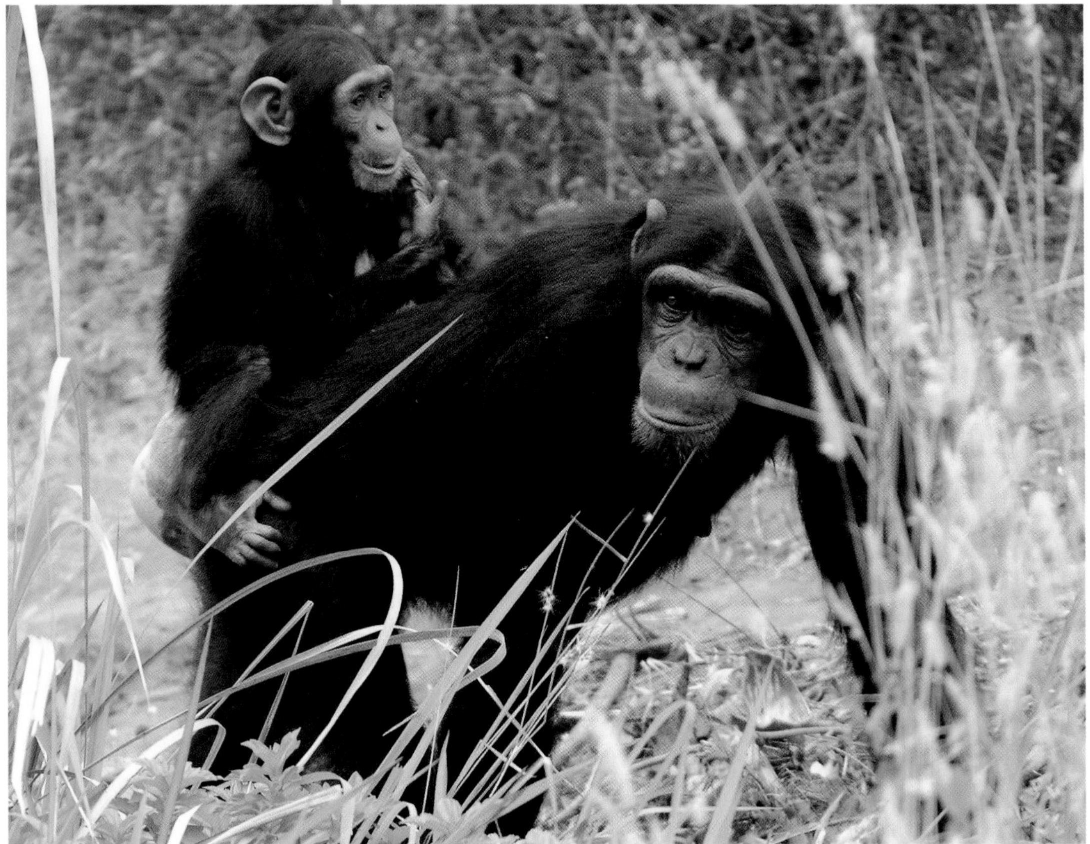

Even our closest ancestors are born more capable than humans are—but the neediness of human babies may present advantages.

THE HELPLESS ADVANTAGE

There are a few theories as to why human babies are born "early" compared to other animals. For one thing, our complicated brains take a long time to develop. But carrying around a baby is a big burden on the mother. It may be more **efficient** for humans to look after helpless babies than for women to stay pregnant for almost two years.

Some researchers suspect there is even more to it. Humans are extremely social animals, and our ability to work together is a vital survival skill. (After all, you can't make Cheez Whiz alone.) The ability to function in groups begins with our relationship to our parents.

Because human babies are so helpless, they need a lot of attention and care. This care creates a bond between adults and children. Back in caveman times, parents who were bonded to their children would have been more likely to save those children from saber-tooth tigers. We also know that the more interaction babies have with adults, the quicker their brains develop. That means that the parental bond gives an intellectual advantage to humans, as well as a social one.

Taking care of helpless infants may actually make the *parents* smarter, too. Our ancient ancestors were constantly in danger, constantly searching for food and shelter . . . all of which is much harder if you are also carrying a helpless baby around. So, at first glance, having a baby might seem like a disadvantage. But some researchers now believe that keeping a baby alive also encouraged problem-solving skills. For instance, a mother might think, "Uh-oh, how do I get the baby away from that tiger over there." Though this is still a theory, it's possible that child rearing might have given early humans an intellectual advantage over other animals.

Babies know that they are dependent on their caregivers for survival. This is where separation anxiety comes in. As their brains develop, babies begin to realize that there is a possibility of their

EDUCATIONAL VIDEO

Here's a video about child development and separation anxiety.

caregiver going away. Given how helpless babies are, it's understandable that this realization might be upsetting! But even if it's no fun, it's an important stage of development.

STEP BY STEP

Experts in child development have identified a series of **milestones** that children should meet as they grow. (See page 21 for more on what milestones are.) For example, babies should be making facial expressions like smiling and frowning by around four months—that's called a social milestone, because it relates to communication. Babies should be able to

Babies don't realize that the image in the mirror is themselves and not some other baby.

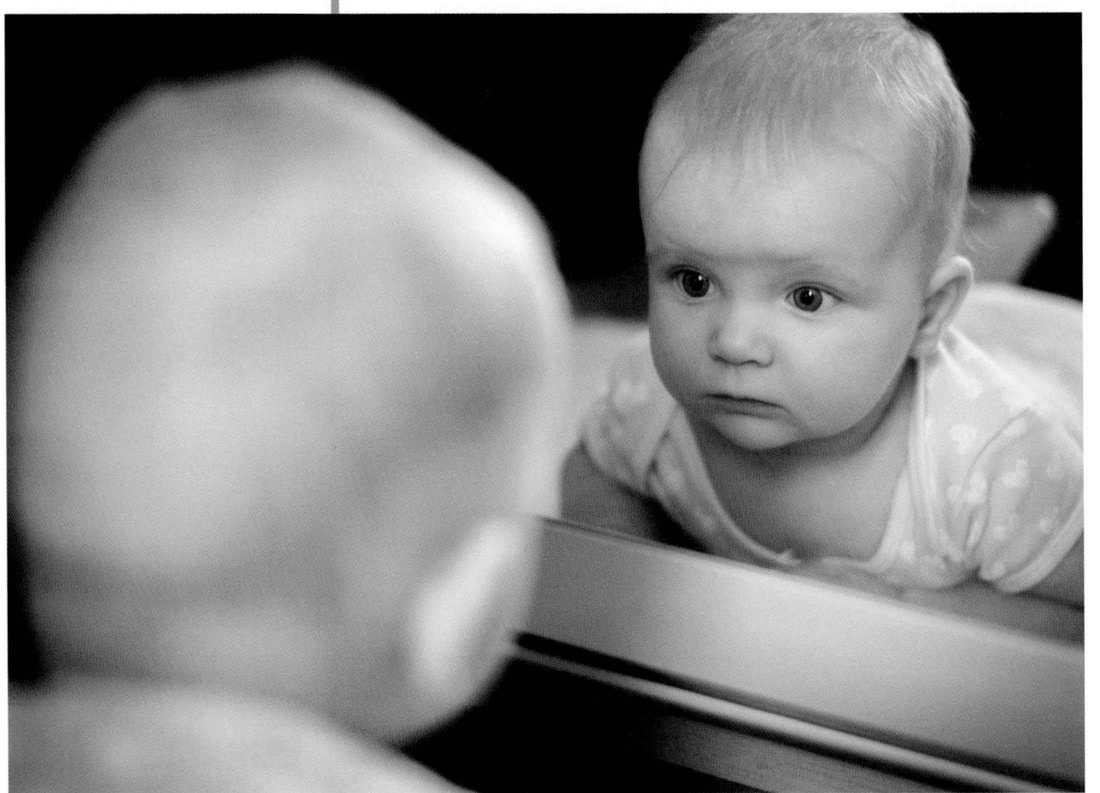

UNDERSTANDING MILESTONES

It might seem confusing that, on the one hand, we say that all people are unique, but on the other hand, we also say that there are certain milestones every child is supposed to meet. There are a few things to understand about milestones.

First, milestones were not invented overnight. Our understanding of child development has evolved over many years of study. So while it's true that every baby is unique, it's also true that we know a lot about babies *in general*.

Second, milestones are more like guideposts than rules. Not every child will meet every milestone at the same moment. In fact, some babies skip right past certain milestones to meet other ones. A perfect example is the babbling we call "baby talk." Some babies start trying to talk when they are only a few months old. Others don't do much babbling at all, but they start talking in short sentences at about two years old. Talking later is not necessarily a problem; for some reason, certain babies just don't bother with babbling.

However, we do know—due to all those years of observation—that talking later *can* sometimes be a symptom of developmental problems. So if a baby seems "off" when it comes to speech milestones, a pediatrician will want to consider whether this is a symptom that needs to be addressed. It may not be! But milestones provide caregivers with hints of what to look for as children grow.

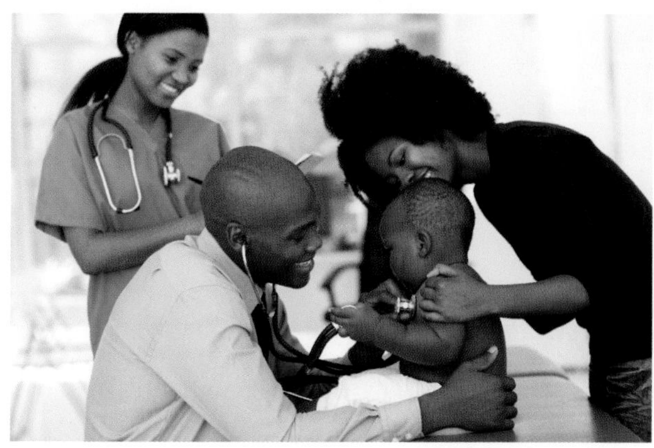

Regular check-ups are important to monitor not only babies' health, but their developmental milestones as well.

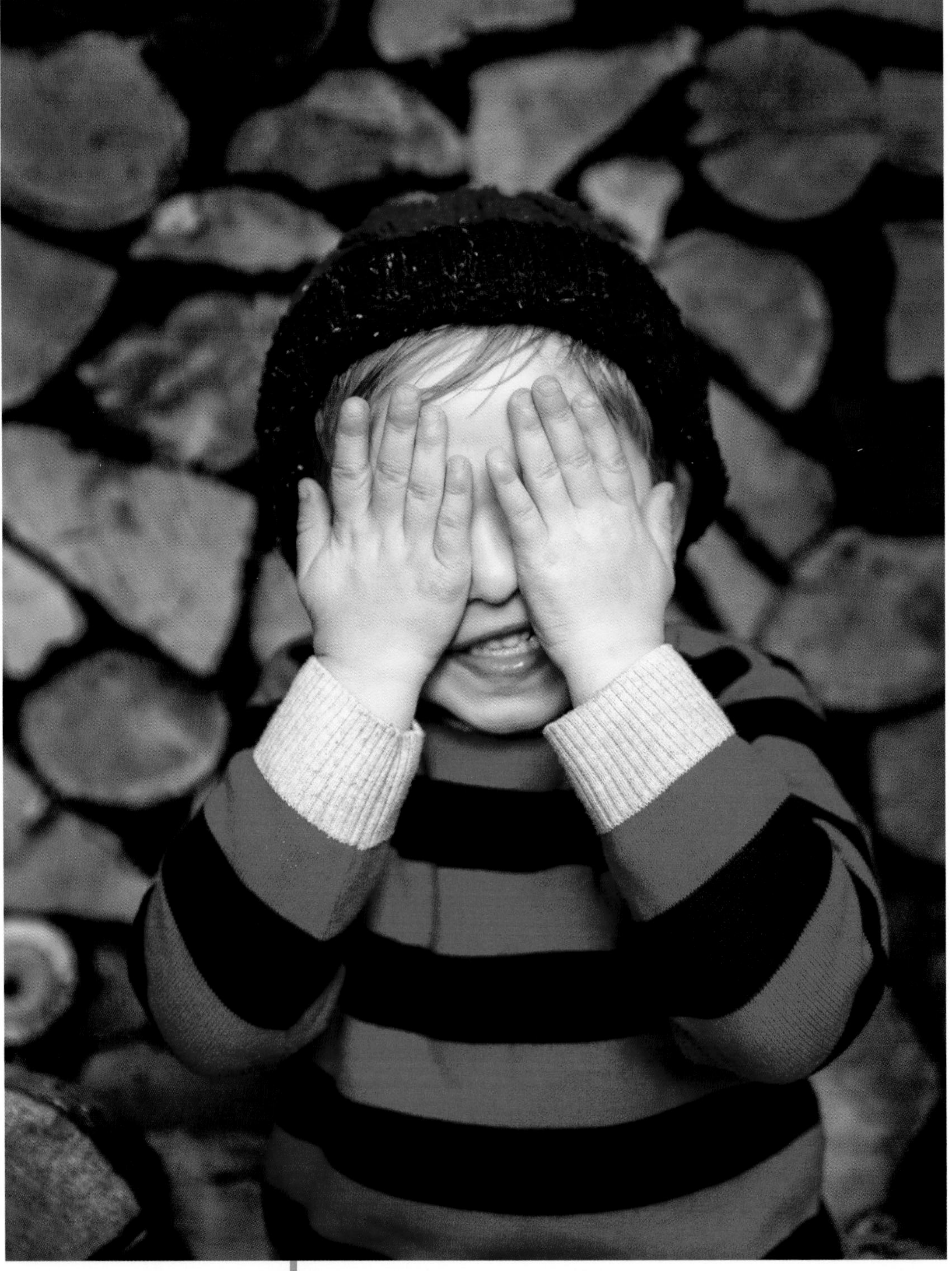

stand by about nine months—that's a motor skill, or physical milestone.

There are also important **cognitive** milestones. An important one, odd as this might sound, is when a baby realizes that he or she is an individual, separate from everybody else. In other words, when a baby realizes that "me" and "you" are two different concepts. When babies are first born, they do not have a sense of themselves as separate from their caregivers. There is no "me" and "you" for a newborn baby.

You might wonder how researchers were able to figure this out. In an experiment called "the mirror test," researchers used mirrors to find out if babies were able to recognize themselves in the reflections. What they found was that babies need to be at least a year old in order to understand that they are looking at themselves in the mirror and not some other baby. (Researchers now use similar tests to figure out which animals are aware of themselves as individuals.) This realization, when it occurs, is an early step toward understanding the difference between "me" and "you."

Another step is the understanding of *object permanence*. Object permanence is the idea that people, places, and things continue to exist even when you are not looking at them. Sounds obvious, right? Well sure, it's obvious to you now, but you were about a year old before you truly understood it. Newborn babies don't even understand that their own bodies continue to exist all the time. The next time you get to

Opposite: Peek-a-boo has been described as the first "joke" that babies learn, because it plays with the idea of object permanence.

see a very young baby, watch how amazed he is every time he "finds" his hands or feet. That's because the baby doesn't understand object permanence.

A psychologist named Jean Piaget conducted a famous experiment in which he showed a toy to a baby, then covered the toy with a blanket. Piaget discovered that it doesn't occur to babies to look for the toy underneath the blanket until they are nearly a year old.

FEAR OF LOSS

Understanding the difference between "me" and "you" is an important milestone. But it does have a dark side. If you and I are separate individuals,

Typically, little kids grow out of their separation anxiety and realize that preschool is actually fun.

CULTURE AND SEPARATION ANXIETY

In this chapter we described separation anxiety as a normal phase of a child's development. But it's important to understand that just because something is "normal" for us, that doesn't mean it is normal for all people everywhere.

Western culture—meaning, the way we live here in North America, plus in most parts of Europe, Australia, and so on—puts a big emphasis on independence. Children are encouraged to be on their own as much as possible. Even tiny babies spend long periods alone when they are sleeping—often in their own cribs and in their own rooms.

Not all cultures view infancy this way. There are many cultures where babies are almost never away from their mothers for the entire first year of life. This does *not* mean that anxiety doesn't exist in those places. In fact, childhood anxiety seems to happen regardless of culture. However, cultural factors can affect when the anxiety occurs and what causes it.

For example, a 1998 study reported that Israeli children who were raised in a **communal** environment known as a *kibbutz* seemed to have less separation anxiety than children in Western cultures. Children on a kibbutz are used to being taken care of by different people in the community, so they don't get as upset if their specific parent is not around. However, these same children showed more fear of strangers than Western kids. This might be because on a kibbutz, little kids are not as used to seeing faces they don't recognize.

that means if you go away, I will be alone. And if a caregiver is a separate being, that means the caregiver could go away, possibly forever.

BROTHERS AND SISTERS

When people talk about separation anxiety, they usually focus on a young child separating from an adult. But that's not the only kind of transition that happens. It is also a big adjustment for little kids when their big brothers or sisters start school.

Little kids miss their siblings a lot—it's just not as much fun without them around to play with! And many times they worry just as much about their safety as they do their parents' safety. If you have a little brother or sister who is upset about you going to school, the tips in this chapter can be helpful in your situation, too.

What makes things worse is that babies have no understanding of time. You can't tell a baby, "I'll be back in five minutes" and expect him to understand what "five minutes" means. This is why periods of separation—such as bedtime or day care or even just leaving the room—can be upsetting.

As kids get a bit older—usually between two and three—they start to understand the passage of time. They realize that there's no need to get upset when Mom goes to the bathroom, because she'll only be gone for a few minutes. They also develop a better ability to remember what happened earlier. Once little kids can remember that Dad came home from work yesterday and the day before, they will have more faith that he will come back today, too. Indeed, there are a lot of songs and stories written for toddlers on the theme of "Mom [or Dad] always comes back."

For some kids, the separation anxiety phase is not a big deal. Maybe they get a little upset when Mom goes to work, but they quickly get over it. Doctors used to worry that babies who didn't have separation anxiety weren't well attached to their parents. However, this is no longer a common view. These days, we believe that separation anxiety depends on the temperament of the individual. Some babies are simply more or less anxious than others.

As we've said, separation anxiety is a normal phase for kids to go through. But there are still things parents and siblings can do to help make the phase easier. So if you have a young, anxious brother or sister, check out some suggestions in chapter four about what to do. But first, let's look at what can sometimes happen if separation anxiety does not fade away on schedule, or if it returns unexpectedly.

Find out more about milestones in child development. Make a chart with three categories—social, physical, and cognitive—and list dates and milestones that are typically expected in the first year of life.

TEXT-DEPENDENT QUESTIONS

1. What are some theories about why human babies are so helpless?
2. What are milestones?
3. What is object permanence?

CHAPTER THREE

PROBLEMS WITH SEPARATION

WORDS TO UNDERSTAND

accommodating: giving in to someone's wishes.

context: the larger situation in which an event takes place.

impairment: here, something that's damaging.

inappropriate: wrong in a particular situation.

persistent: happening over a period of time.

remission: a temporary recovery from an illness.

Let's imagine a boy in the fifth grade. He is having trouble at school because he can't stop worrying about his dad. The boy keeps picturing his dad being in a car crash or getting shot. The terrible thoughts won't stop, and the boy gets more and more upset. The only thing that makes him feel better is seeing his dad and being around him all the time. We might wonder if this boy has separation anxiety disorder.

But what if the boy's mom recently died of cancer, leaving him and his dad all alone? Or what if his dad is a soldier, deployed overseas? In those cases, we would not be so quick to say he has separation anxiety disorder. He probably needs some help learning how to manage his worry. But his feelings are a direct response to difficult events in his life. Worrying about your parent's safety is not unreasonable if you've got a good reason to do so.

Or consider a girl who is in the sixth grade who cries every morning when she gets on the bus for school. In our culture, we believe that sixth grade is "too old" for someone to be crying about leaving home. First grade, sure. But by the sixth grade, we expect someone to have gotten used to the idea of getting on a school bus. So we might wonder if the girl in our example has separation anxiety disorder.

And the answer is, she might! But what if she explained that when she gets to school, she knows she will be beaten up or humiliated by the other kids? If you know that you are going to be bullied when you get to school, wanting to cry when you see a school bus actually makes sense. It is a sad and upsetting response, for sure, but it is an appropriate response.

Getting upset when you have to be away from your family is not necessarily a "disorder"; it might be a natural reaction to whatever is going on in your life.

This is why **context** is so important when it comes to mental disorders. A person with separation anxiety disorder feels very upset about being apart from an attachment figure. The person's worry may not have a clear cause. Or it might have a cause, but the *level* of anxiety does not make sense given the person's age. Or it might continue for a long time and have a strongly negative impact on the person's life. Many factors need to be considered in figuring out whether someone has separation anxiety disorder or some other type of problem.

DEFINING SEPARATION ANXIETY DISORDER

In order to figure out whether someone has a particular mental disorder, doctors use a guidebook called the *Diagnostic and Statistical Manual of Mental Disorders* (*DSM*). The *DSM* explains in detail what makes separation anxiety disorder different from normal childhood separation anxiety.

First, separation anxiety disorder involves fear that is "developmentally **inappropriate**." That's doctor-speak for behavior that doesn't line up with someone's age or level of maturity. If you feel nervous before leaving home for summer camp, there is nothing developmentally inappropriate about that. Separation anxiety disorder involves fear that goes beyond what would be expected at a particular age.

EDUCATIONAL VIDEO

Here is a video about the medical condition called separation anxiety disorder.

Anxiety disorders involve persistent, strong feelings that aren't developmentally appropriate and that interfere with regular life.

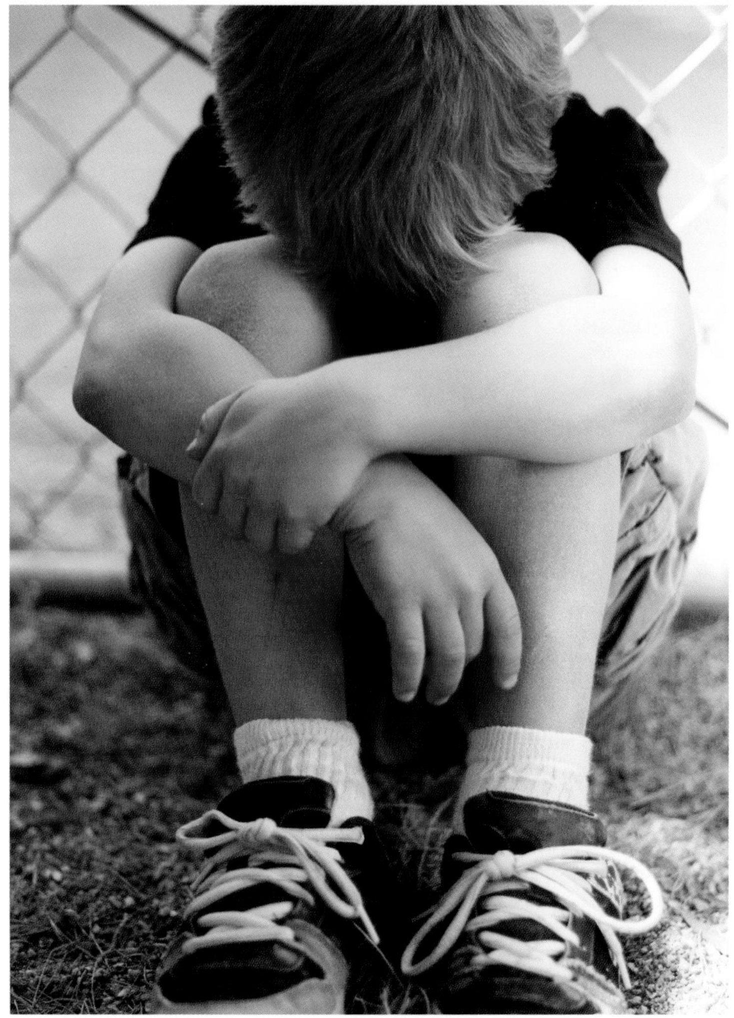

The next *DSM* criteria is "excessive fear and anxiety." The word *excessive* is really important. Separation anxiety disorder is not just feeling a little anxious about leaving home. The feelings have to be more intense than that. Maybe the person feels physically ill (headache, nausea, vomiting) if she has to leave home. Maybe she can't stop worrying about being kidnapped or somehow taken away from her attachment figure. Some people with separation anxiety disorder get very upset when they even *think* about their attachment figure not being around. Regular nightmares about separation are also a potential symptom of the disorder.

OTHER ISSUES

The symptoms of separation anxiety disorder are very similar to a variety of other anxiety-related problems. That's why it's so important that people not diagnose themselves with mental disorders. Doctors and therapists are trained to help patients figure out what the real source of a particular problem might be. It's very easy to mistake one type of issue for another.

A few of the other problems that might look like separation anxiety disorder include:

- **adjustment disorder:** intense stress or panic in reaction to a particular life change (like moving or parents getting divorced); can make kids more "clingy" than normal.
- **agoraphobia:** an extreme fear of open spaces; people feel anxious when they are away from home.
- **depression:** a mood disorder that may make someone reluctant to leave the house.
- **post-traumatic stress disorder (PTSD):** anxiety in reaction to violence or other traumatic events; fear for the safety of loved ones may be related to PTSD.
- **social anxiety disorder:** intense fear of certain kinds of interactions with others; can cause kids to refuse to go to school or meet new people.

But notice that word we just used: *regular*. That's the next part of the *DSM* definition, although the *DSM* uses the word **persistent**. A person who has one nightmare about the death of a parent does not have separation anxiety disorder. Nor does a child who acts very "clingy" for a few days and then stops. To be considered a disorder, the upset feelings have to get in the way of daily life for an extended period of time (usually a month or more).

This idea of getting in the way of daily life is also important. The *DSM* calls this **impairment**. Someone with separation anxiety disorder might want to go play at a friend's house, but the anxiety about leaving home prevents him from doing it. A kid might find it impossible to fall asleep in her own bed or deal with school all day, just because the separation anxiety is so bad.

The final part of *DSM*'s definition is that the anxiety can't be explained by some other factor. Consider the kids mentioned at the beginning of this chapter: both have symptoms that might look like separation anxiety disorder, but their fears can be explained by other factors. For example, routines are very important to kids with the developmental disorder called autism. If Mom doesn't come home from work on time, a kid with autism might get really upset. But that's not necessarily separation anxiety—in that case, the upset feelings are caused by the interruption of an expected routine.

Leaving home for college is a life event that may trigger some separation anxiety.

CAUSES OF SEPARATION ANXIETY DISORDER

A Greek philosopher named Heraclitus remarked that "change is the only constant in life." Sometimes change is exciting, such as when we start new schools or jobs, or when we move into a new house in a new neighborhood. But sometimes change is terrible, such as when parents get divorced, or when people we love move far away. Whether the changes are good or bad, they usually bring a certain amount of anxiety.

Most of the time, we get used to new situations. The anxiety fades. But sometimes it doesn't work out that way. Big life changes are a potential source of separation anxiety disorder.

Sometimes parents need to learn how to respond to their kids' anxiety.

Frequently (although not always), kids with separation anxiety disorder have their first bout of it around the time they start either nursery school or kindergarten. Most kids experience a little shyness or worry at first, but they tend to get over it pretty quickly. But for kids with separation anxiety, spending time away from their attachment figure is extremely painful and upsetting. Frequently, the disorder will get better for a little while (this is called **remission**), and then it will come back when a new life change occurs.

TREATMENTS

If the fear of being away from an attachment figure is keeping someone from going to school or making friends, it might be time to get outside help.

The most common form of treatment is called cognitive-behavioral therapy (CBT). The word *cognitive* relates to how we think, and the word *behavioral* relates to how we act. Therapists help kids understand the situations that cause (or "trigger") their separation anxiety. Then they practice a technique called *exposure*, which involves working gradually toward feeling better about the idea of separation. Kids learn coping strategies to get through their anxious feelings. That might sound easy, but it is definitely not! Anxious feelings are very real to the people who have them. It takes time and practice to respond to the feelings in a calmer way.

Parents have a big role to play in helping their kids with separation anxiety disorder. It is common for parents to accept and just live with their child's anxiety without realizing they are doing it—therapists call this **accommodating** the anxiety. Oftentimes, parents also need to learn new ways of responding to anxious situations. It's also very important that parents understand the anxiety cycle, learn alternatives to accommodating, praise their kids' progress, and reinforce the good habits being practiced in therapy.

RESEARCH PROJECT

Find out more about CBT. Make a list of some specific exercises someone in CBT might use in order to control anxiety. (You might start with the information provided by the West Virginia University Students' Center of Health; see Further Reading section for the URL.)

TEXT-DEPENDENT QUESTIONS

1. Why does context matter when it comes to separation anxiety?
2. How does the *DSM* define separation anxiety disorder?
3. What kind of treatment is most often used?

CHAPTER FOUR

DEALING WITH SEPARATION

As we've said, separation anxiety is a typical stage of childhood. It is inevitable to a certain extent. However, there are things that parents and families can do to help make things easier. In the case of separation anxiety disorder, parents and family have a huge role to play in helping the person overcome challenges.

intentionally: on purpose.

reassurance: lessening someone's fears.

reinforce: to strengthen something.

HELPING LITTLE ONES

The first step in helping a little one with separation anxiety is understanding what's going on. The child is not **intentionally** being difficult—separation anxiety is a natural response in toddlers. Once caregivers, whether parents or someone else, have understood and accepted this, they can make choices to help the child feel more secure. Yes, there may be crying at first. But it's better to accept the fact that some crying is unavoidable—and, remember, normal—and face up to it. Listed below are some things that can help.

- *Don't sneak out.* Many caregivers would like to avoid the crying entirely, and some try to

Here is a video that could be shown to little kids with separation anxiety.

accomplish this by leaving their children without saying goodbye. This is a mistake. Try and see it from the child's perspective. If a family member sneaks away, disappearing for no clear reason—the lesson the child learns is that people can simply vanish at any given moment. Sneaking out teaches that adults are actually not trustworthy. This can have the exact opposite effect of what the parents intend, making the child more anxious rather than less.

Instead, family members should say goodbye clearly and calmly. Remind the child of where you are going, and reassure him or her that you will be back at a particular point in time. Sometimes developing a predictable goodbye routine can be helpful. Toddlers will not follow much of this at first, but with repetition, they will start to understand.

- *Stay calm.* Kids pick up a lot from the tone that family members use with one another. If the people around are calm and reassuring, in time the toddler will start to feel more calm also.
- *Keep it simple.* Although it's important to say goodbye, it's also important to avoid being too dramatic about it. Little kids don't need long, drawn-out goodbyes, and they also don't need detailed explanations. Sometimes parents want to talk about the complex reasons for their actions, or how this is the

best day care in the city, or what have you. But it's not helpful to the little one. Short and sweet goodbyes are best.

- *Make it familiar.* Whenever possible, kids should spend time with whoever is going to watch them before the actual separation happens. For example, if a family has hired a new babysitter, it's a good idea to let the younger kids meet the babysitter before the big night out.
- *Remember the little things.* Keeping a small comfort object from home is a way for nervous kids to feel connected. Some parents put notes in lunch boxes, to remind their kids that they are loved. Having a specific goodbye ritual—like a "secret" handshake or a pattern of two kisses and one hug—can also help mark a separation in a positive way.
- *Have distractions ready.* If you are a big brother or sister to a toddler, this is where you can be super helpful. After the parent has said goodbye and left, it's time to immediately change the mood with an engaging activity. Don't let the little one dwell too long on the person who just left. Playing a game, curling up with a favorite book, or watching a video together are ways to provide **reassurance** and, importantly, distraction. (A cookie is also nice, but not required.)

When dropping a child off at preschool, a loving-but-brief goodbye is usually best.

GETTING PAST SEPARATION ANXIETY

There is no benefit to sneaking around, fibbing, or pretending that separations never happen. There is also no benefit to a constant obsessive focus on separation. By attempting to be helpful, family members sometimes actually make the situation worse.

One common mistake is when parents start encouraging the child to avoid situations that might cause stress. They mean well—like all parents, they want their child to be happy. But if a parent decides that a particular situation—such as school, a friend's house, a trip to the mall, and the like—is too scary and should be avoided, the child will think, "Wow, if Mom wants to avoid that, I better avoid it!" This is called an *anxiety cycle*: a child has separation anxiety, so the parents try to avoid separations, but the avoidance only serves to **reinforce** the idea that separation is bad.

Another pitfall is when parents communicate—either with words or actions—their own anxiety to their kids. This is another cycle. The child's anxiety causes the parents' anxiety, the child can sense the parents' anxiety, and this makes the child fear separations more than ever. Sometimes parents enjoy being needed by their children. And it is definitely nice to be needed! But it can lead to parents, usually unintentionally, encouraging their young children to be clingy.

Instead, family members of people with separation anxiety disorder should gently encourage their loved one to branch out and try different activities. A therapist can help family members figure out how much encouragement is the right amount.

RESEARCH PROJECT

Read more, either in books or online, about separation anxiety in little kids. Based on what you've learned, make something—a comic, a story, or even a song—that teaches little kids about how to get over separation anxiety.

TEXT-DEPENDENT QUESTIONS

1. Why is it a bad idea to leave without saying goodbye?
2. What are some tips to help ease separation anxiety?
3. How are big brothers and sisters affected by separation anxiety?

FURTHER READING

Eisen, Andrew R., and Linda B. Engler. *Helping Your Child Overcome Separation Anxiety or School Refusal.* Oakland, CA: New Harbinger, 2006.

Hurley, Katie. "Helping Preschoolers Cope with Separation Anxiety." *PBS Parents*, September 8, 2015. http://www.pbs.org/parents/expert-tips-advice/2015/09/helping-preschoolers-cope-separation-anxiety/.

KidsHealth. "Separation Anxiety." http://kidshealth.org/en/parents/sep-anxiety.html.

Konnikova, Maria. "Why Are Babies So Dumb If Humans Are So Smart?" *New Yorker*, September 7, 2016. http://www.newyorker.com/science/maria-konnikova/why-are-babies-so-dumb-if-humans-are-so-smart.

WebMD. "Separation Anxiety Disorder in Children." http://www.webmd.com/children/guide/separation-anxiety#1.

West Virginia University Students' Center of Health. "CBT Strategies for Anxiety Relief." http://well.wvu.edu/articles/cbt_strategies_for_anxiety_relief.

EDUCATIONAL VIDEOS

Chapter One: Beating Anxiety. "Dealing with Separation Anxiety in Teens." https://youtu.be/dRFgSpJz-K4.

Chapter Two: Parentchannel.tv. "Separation Anxiety." https://youtu.be/58khDBvteTs.

Chapter Three: AnxietyBC. "Child Separation Anxiety Disorder." https://www.anxietybc.com/resources/video/child-separation-anxiety-disorder.

Chapter Four: TeenMentalHealth.org. "Tom Has Separation Anxiety Disorder." https://youtu.be/jEkFp0Ux4OQ.

SERIES GLOSSARY

adaptive: a helpful response to a particular situation.

bias: a feeling against a particular thing or idea.

biofeedback: monitoring of bodily functions with the goal of learning to control those functions.

cognitive: relating to the brain and thought.

comorbid: when one illness or disorder is present alongside another one.

context: the larger situation in which an event takes place.

diagnose: to identify an illness or disorder.

exposure: having contact with something.

extrovert: a person who enjoys being with others.

harassment: picking on another person frequently and deliberately.

hypnosis: creating a state of consciousness where someone is awake but highly open to suggestion.

inhibitions: feelings that restricts what we do or say.

introvert: a person who prefers being alone.

irrational: baseless; something that's not connected to reality.

melatonin: a substance that helps the body regulate sleep.

milestone: an event that marks a stage in development.

motivating: something that makes you want to work harder.

occasional: from time to time; not often.

panic attack: sudden episode of intense, overwhelming fear.

paralyzing: something that makes you unable to move (can refer to physical movement as well as emotions).

peers: people who are roughly the same age as you.

perception: what we see and believe to be true.

persistent: continuing for a noticeable period.

phobia: extreme fear of a particular thing.

preventive: keeping something from happening.

probability: the likelihood that a particular thing will happen.

psychological: having to do with the mind and thoughts.

rational: based on a calm understanding of facts, rather than emotion.

sedative: a type of drug that slows down bodily processes, making people feel relaxed or even sleepy.

self-conscious: overly aware of yourself, to the point that it makes you awkward.

serotonin: a chemical in the brain that is important in moods.

stereotype: an oversimplified idea about a type of person that may not be true for any given individual.

stigma: a sense of shame or disgrace associated with a particular state of being.

stimulant: a group of substances that speed up bodily processes.

subconscious: thoughts and feelings you have but may not be aware of.

syndrome: a condition.

treatable: describes a medical condition that can be healed.

upheaval: a period of great change or uncertainty.

INDEX

ABOUT THE ADVISOR

Anne S. Walters is Clinical Associate Professor of Psychiatry and Human Behavior at the Alpert Medical School of Brown University. She is also Chief Psychologist for Bradley Hospital. She is actively involved in teaching activities within the Clinical Psychology Training Programs of the Alpert Medical School and serves as Child Track Seminar Co-Coordinator. Dr. Walters completed her undergraduate work at Duke University, graduate school at Georgia State University, internship at UTexas Health Science Center, and postdoctoral fellowship at Brown University.

ABOUT THE AUTHOR

H. W. Poole is a writer and editor of books for young people, including the sets, *Families Today* and *Mental Illnesses and Disorders: Awareness and Understanding* (Mason Crest). She created the *Horrors of History* series (Charlesbridge) and the *Ecosystems* series (Facts On File). She has also been responsible for many critically acclaimed reference books, including *Political Handbook of the World* (CQ Press) and the *Encyclopedia of Terrorism* (SAGE). She was coauthor and editor of *The History of the Internet* (ABC-CLIO), which won the 2000 American Library Association RUSA award.

PHOTO CREDITS

Cover (clockwise): Shutterstock/Sean Locke Photography; iStock/ XiXinXing; iStock/ MivPiv; Shutterstock/Tomsickova Tatyana
iStock: 8: THEPALMER; 10 Kouptsova; 11 valbar; 13 max-kegfire; 14 vasiliki; 16 AtnoYdur; 18 dangdumrong; 20 angiii; 21 michaeljung; 22 wundervisuals; 24 FatCamera; 32 stray_cat; 35 XiXinXing; 36 carterdayne
Shutterstock: 28 Jamie Hooper; 30 alexkatkov; 38 kryzhov; 42 stockphoto mania